Disney's

Winnie the Pooh's Friendly Adventures

A Read-Aloud Storybook Collection

MOUSE WORKS

Find us at www.DisneyBooks.com for more Mouse Works fun!

Printed in the United States of America.
Based on the Pooh stories by A. A. Milne
(copyright The Pooh Properties Trust).
First Edition
10 9 8 7 6 5 4 3 2 1
This book is set in Goudy.
ISBN: 0-7364-0107-5

Contents

4

Pooh's Sticky Situation

"Oh bother," sighed Pooh. "My tummy is very rumbly, but my honey is all gone."

Now, *honey* rhymes with *bunny*, so Pooh Bear set off to visit his good friend Rabbit. Rabbit always had honey at his house.

"You're just in time for lunch," said Rabbit as Pooh squeezed in through the front door.

Pooh sat down at the table and ate . . . and ate . . . and ate some more. "Thank you for the honey," Pooh said at last in a rather sticky voice.

But as he tried to leave, Pooh's big, round tummy got in the way. No matter how much Rabbit pushed, poked, and shoved, Pooh didn't budge.

"I must find Christopher Robin," cried Rabbit as he ran out the back door.

"Silly old bear," said Christopher Robin. He and Rabbit tugged and pulled, but Pooh stayed stuck.

"There's only one thing to do," said Christopher Robin. "We must wait for you to get thin again." So they waited.

When Eeyore saw what had happened, he said, "This could take days. Or weeks . . . or maybe even months."

"Oh bother," said Pooh. Rabbit agreed.

That night Gopher paid a hungry Pooh a visit. "Time for my midnight snack," said Gopher.

Rabbit showed up just in time. "No!" he cried. "Not one drop of honey for Pooh." Then he put up a sign that read:

DO NOT FEED THE BEAR.

Time passed, but Pooh stayed stuck. Then one day, it happened. Pooh moved, but just a little bit.

15

Pooh's friends gathered around to help Pooh get unstuck. They pushed and pulled, and pushed a little more. . . .

Pop! Pooh flew out of Rabbit's doorway and crashed into a hollow tree. "Stuck again," Eeyore sighed.

"Don't worry," Christopher Robin called to Pooh. "We'll get you right out of that tree."

Pooh was in no hurry. There was honey above him, below him, and all around him. "Take your time, Christopher Robin," Pooh called down. "Take your time!"

19

Special Friends

It makes me glad to make up hums.

It makes me glad when Christmas comes.

20

It makes me glad when bees make honey.

It makes me glad when days are sunny.

It makes me glad to win a game.

It makes me glad that Pooh's my name.

I saved the best one for the end.

It makes me glad that you're my friend!

24

Unbouncing Tigger

Rabbit was working in his garden. Suddenly . . . *BOING!* He was bounced flat on his back.

Rabbit looked up at Tigger and asked, "Won't you ever stop bouncing?"

"Nope!" said Tigger. "Bouncing is what Tiggers do best."

Rabbit wanted to *unbounce* Tigger. He told Pooh and Piglet, "We're going to take Tigger for a walk, and then we'll lose him!"

Pooh frowned. "Losing someone doesn't seem like a friendly thing to do," he said.

"Don't worry," Rabbit said. "We'll find him again. But by then he'll be a less bouncy Tigger. An oh-Rabbit-am-I-glad-to-see-you Tigger."

So one misty morning, the four friends took a walk. *Boing-boing!* Tigger bounced circles around his friends and then he bounced right out of sight!

"Now is our chance to lose Tigger!" said Rabbit, squeezing into a hollow log. Tigger bounced back and called for his pals, but he couldn't find them.

"Now we can go home," Rabbit decided. But instead of finding home, he kept finding the same sandpit over and over.

Pooh's tummy rumbled. Some honeypots were calling him home, so he and Piglet decided to follow their call. Rabbit hopped off on his own.

Pooh soon bumped into Tigger. When Tigger found out that Rabbit was lost, he said, "Tiggers never get lost!" And he bounced off to the rescue.

Poor Rabbit was feeling scared and alone when Tigger finally appeared. Rabbit was now a rescued Rabbit, a lost-and-found Rabbit. But most of all, he was an oh-Tigger-am-I-glad-to-see-you Rabbit!

Pooh's Friendly Hums

Some bears growl,
some bears snort,
but Pooh Bear is
the humming sort.
Here are some hums about his friends.
Pooh hopes you like them from starts to ends!

Eeyore's gray,
although it's true,
he's frequently
a little blue.

Rabbit is so
very busy.
Watching him
makes Pooh Bear dizzy.

Rum-tee-tiddle-tum
tiddle-tum-too,
when Kanga jumps,
so does Roo.

Wise Owl answers all Pooh's questions
(he even adds his own suggestions)
but when he gets the answer out,
Pooh's forgotten what he asked about.

Piglet is so
very small,
sometimes he can't be
seen at all!

Gopher is a friend
who may or may not be around.
Pooh really can't be sure
without peeking underground.

Bouncing higher
than all the rest
is just the thing
Tiggers do best!

Pooh's Grand Adventure

The Search for Christopher Robin

One golden day in the Hundred-Acre Wood, Winnie the Pooh set off to meet Christopher Robin on their special hill.

But today Pooh's friend seemed sad. "Pooh Bear, suppose a tomorrow came and we weren't together?" Christopher Robin asked.

"I'm glad it's tomorrow because then I don't have to think about it today," said Pooh.

"Silly old bear," laughed Christopher Robin.

The next morning when Pooh arrived at the special spot, Christopher Robin was not there. But a large pot of honey with a note was!

Rumble, grumbled Pooh's tummy. "My tummy says this honey is for me," said Pooh, "but this note may say it is for someone else."

Pooh's friends gathered to help him read the note and solve the honey mystery. "Ahem," said Owl. "Christopher Robin has gone to *Skull*!"

"*Skull!*" gasped Tigger. "Are you absoposilutely sure an' certain?"

"What else can S-C-H-O-O-L spell?" Owl demanded.

"How can we rescue Christopher Robin?" Pooh asked. As usual, Owl had the answer. He drew a map with all sorts of spooky spots on it, leading to the spookiest spot of all—Skull Cave.

Owl was soon waving them a cheery farewell. "Toodle-oo! I'll keep a sharp eye out for your return . . . if you do return, of course."

The rescue party's prickly tramp through the Forest of Thorns took them to . . .

the Valley of Flowers (complete with Piglet-napping Flutterbys) . . .

which led to the Screaming Gorge and the Valley of Mists. At last, the friends arrived at a cave so scary and dark, it had to be Skull.

Once inside the cave, a horrible growling erupted from the darkness! The brave rescuers split up to find Christopher Robin more quickly.

But all they found was each other in the Crystal
Cavern, without a sign of Christopher Robin.
The growls grew louder and louder. Suddenly, a
long shadow fell over the cavern.

The shadow was . . . Christopher Robin!
"We saved you from Skull," cheered Pooh.
"Skull? I was at *school*," said Christopher Robin.
"That Owl!" complained Tigger. "I *knew* skull
had another Y in it."

"What about the growls?" squeaked Piglet,
jumping into Pooh's arms as another rumble echoed
through the cave.

"That's the rumbly tummy," said Christopher Robin, smiling, "of a bear who's hungry for honey." Everyone listened again. The growls weren't a bit scary now that they knew where they came from!

Back at home, Pooh and Christopher Robin sat together atop their special hill. "Pooh Bear, will you remember that even if we're apart, I'll always be with you?" Christopher Robin asked.

"Yes, Christopher Robin," Pooh said. "And I'll always be with you, too."